Bear's Christmas Surprise

AlYna

For Nathalie, to whom I have owed
an *H* for a long time.
E.W.

For the sequels to the Queen,
Caitlin, Johnno, and Lucy Rein Sargent.
With love,
P.B.

Published by
Bantam Doubleday Dell Books for Young Readers
a division of
Random House, Inc.
1540 Broadway
New York, New York 10036

Text copyright © 1991 by Elizabeth Winthrop
Illustrations copyright © 1991 by Patience Brewster

Visit us on the Web! www.randomhouse.com

**Educators and librarians, for a variety of teaching tools, visit us at
www.randomhouse.com/teachers**

ISBN: 0-440-41492-X
Reprinted by arrangement with Holiday House, Inc.
Printed in the United States of America
November 1999

10 9 8 7 6 5 4 3 2 1

Bear's Christmas Surprise

ELIZABETH WINTHROP

ILLUSTRATED BY

PATIENCE BREWSTER

A PICTURE YEARLING BOOK

One week before Christmas, Nora told Bear, "I'm going shopping, and Mrs. Duck is coming to baby-sit."

"Goody," said Bear. He liked Mrs. Duck. She had funny floppy feet and a fat fluffy tail. She read stories out loud and drew pictures and played hide-and-seek.

"Here she comes," cried Bear.

"Have fun with Mrs. Duck," Nora said, as she put on her coat. "When I get back, we'll make Christmas cookies."

"Do you promise?" asked Bear.

"I promise," said Nora. "And remember, no peeking at the presents. The best part of Christmas is being surprised."

"Okay," said Bear.

"Do you promise?" asked Nora.

"I promise," said Bear.

"What shall we do first?" Mrs. Duck asked.

"Let's draw a picture," said Bear. "I'm going to draw a train. That's what I want for Christmas most of all."

Mrs. Duck got the crayons out of her bag. She drew a picture of a new hat. On top of the hat, she drew a banana, and a pear and four apples.

Bear drew his train going around a track. The train had a steam engine, a coal car, a boxcar, a flatcar, and a shiny red caboose.

"That's a beautiful train," said Mrs. Duck.

"That's the train I want for Christmas," said Bear.

"And I want this hat," said Mrs. Duck, as she colored in the last apple.

They pinned their pictures on the bulletin board in the kitchen.

"What shall we do now?" asked Mrs. Duck.

"Let's play hide-and-seek," said Bear. "I want to hide first."

Mrs. Duck closed her eyes and began to count. Bear ran and hid in Nora's closet behind her dresses. In the distance, he heard Mrs. Duck call, "Ready or not, here I come."

It was very dark in the closet, so Bear turned on the light. He heard Mrs. Duck bumping around the room. "My," she said to herself. "Bear is a very good hider. He's not under the bed and he's not behind the curtains. Where is he?"

"I bet he's in the bathtub, that clever Bear," Mrs. Duck said. She went out of the room again.

Bear was getting tired. He slid down until his bottom hit something. Bear looked down. He was sitting on a box. A wrapped-up-in-Christmas-paper box.

"Uh-oh," said Bear. "I promised Nora I wouldn't peek at the presents. So I won't.

I'll just sit." He sat on the wrapped-up box and closed his eyes. But Mrs. Duck was taking a very long time.

"This box is very small," said Bear. "Much too small to hold a toy train."

He pushed Nora's dresses away. He saw more wrapped-up boxes.

He picked them up and shook them. One was flat and hard. It felt like a book. One was very small. It rattled a little bit. It sounded like a package of tightly packed crayons. Then Bear picked up his sitting box. It wasn't very heavy. Not heavy enough for a toy train with a steam engine, a coal car, a boxcar, a flatcar, and a shiny red caboose.

Bear felt sick.
He had promised Nora
that he wouldn't peek.

Now he had sneaked
and peeked and rattled
the boxes.

He opened the closet door.
   "Mrs. Duck," he called.
"I don't feel well."
   "Why, there you are," cried
Mrs. Duck. "You are too
good a hider for me."

"I feel sick," said Bear. "I have a stomach-
ache and a headache and my feet feel funny."
"Oh, dear," said Mrs. Duck. "We'd better
put you right to bed."

So Bear crawled into bed. Mrs. Duck tucked him in and took his temperature and brought him a glass of water.

"Nora should be home any minute," said Mrs. Duck.

"I feel very very sick," moaned Bear. He pulled the covers up over his head.

Mrs. Duck read him his favorite book, but Bear couldn't even look at the pictures. He stayed under the covers.

The front door opened. "I'm home," Nora called. But Bear didn't move.

"Bear, where are you?" Nora called. Bear held his breath. He heard Nora and Mrs. Duck whispering together.

"Bear, say good-bye to Mrs. Duck," Nora said.

"Good-bye, Mrs. Duck," Bear said. His voice sounded very small.

"Good-bye, Bear," said Mrs. Duck. "I hope you feel better soon."

Nora tried to lift the covers, but Bear held on tight. He did not want Nora to look at him.

"What's wrong, Bear?" she whispered. "Mrs. Duck says you feel sick."

"I peeked," said Bear, in a very small voice.

"What did you say, Bear?" asked Nora. "I can't hear you."

Bear threw off the covers and sat up in bed. "I sneaked and I peeked and I shook the boxes," Bear cried. "And there was no train." Then he burst into tears.

Nora pulled Bear into her lap and rocked him back and forth.

"I didn't mean to," Bear said. "We were playing hide-and-seek."

"I know," said Nora. She held out her big white handkerchief, and Bear blew his nose.

"You said the best part about Christmas is being surprised," said Bear. "And now I know there's no toy train."

"Maybe Santa Claus will put a train in your stocking," said Nora.

"My train is too big to fit into a stocking," said Bear. "Besides, Santa Claus won't bring a train to a sneaking, peeking Bear like me."

"But now the sneaking, peeking Bear is a sad and sorry Bear," said Nora. "And Nora loves him very much.

Let's go bake some Christmas cookies.

That will cheer you up.''

Nora put the sugar and the butter in a big bowl. Bear stirred and mashed.

"What did you do with Mrs. Duck?" Nora asked.

"We drew those pictures," said Bear. "I drew the train and Mrs. Duck drew the hat. That's what she wants for Christmas. Can we get it for her?"

"What a good idea, Bear," said Nora. "Tomorrow we'll go to the hat store and see what we can find."

Bear felt better. He made six star cookies and twelve tree cookies, and then he sprinkled them all with red and green sugar.

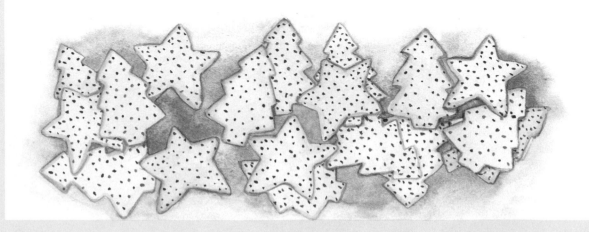

On Christmas morning, Bear tiptoed into the living room. There, under the tree, he found a surprise . . .

. . . and so did Mrs. Duck!